Disney's
Winnie the Pooh
Hooray for Teamwork

When you have a job to do,

The way to get it done

Is work together as a team.

It's really much more fun!

Every once in a while, a "Perfect-for-Playing-Tag" day comes along in the Hundred-Acre Wood. And this just happened to be one of those days.

"You're it!" Christopher Robin laughed, tagging Pooh.

"Oh, bother. Me again?" Pooh sighed, sitting down. "My legs are too hungry to run anymore. Isn't it about dinner time?"

"I guess it is getting kind of late," Christopher Robin said.

"Time to call it quits," Rabbit agreed.

"I'll get my jacket," Christopher Robin said. "I left it over on the bush."

But when Christopher Robin got to the bush, his jacket wasn't there!

"I'm sure I put it here earlier," Christopher Robin said.
"Was it a blue jacket with gold buttons?" Eeyore asked.
"Yes, it was!" Christopher Robin said. "Have you seen it?"
"No," Eeyore said, shaking his head.

"I saw it hanging right there earlier," Owl said, pointing.
"Well, it's definitely not there now," Rabbit said.
"It's a mystery," Pooh said, scratching his head.
"Very suspicerous!" Tigger said.

"How will I ever find it?" Christopher Robin asked.

"We'll help you!" everyone chorused at once.

"Thank you," Christopher Robin said with a smile. "If we work together as a team, I know we can find my jacket."

Tigger started by bouncing Roo high up among the tree branches to look for it.

"See anything up there, Buddy Boy?" Tigger asked.

"No, but this sure is fun!" Roo cried.

Down on the ground, Pooh searched inside every honey pot in the Hundred-Acre Wood.

While Pooh searched, his friend Piglet did his best to hold onto Pooh and keep him from falling in.

But as Pooh searched inside a particularly big honey pot, he tumbled headfirst right into it.

"I say," cried Owl, who happened to be flying overhead. "A stuck bear in quite a bit of stickiness."

"I'd better check this one again," Pooh said, emerging from the big pot, dripping with honey. "Or maybe you'd like to check it, Piglet," he said politely. "You can have a little smackerel while you're in there."

Meanwhile, Eeyore helped as his friend Rabbit tried to get into a very small hole.

"I have a feeling that jacket is in there," Rabbit insisted.

"All right, so it's not in here," Rabbit's muffled voice admitted from inside the hole. Rabbit held tight onto Eeyore's tail as Eeyore strained to pull him out. "We work well together, don't you think?" Rabbit asked a weary Eeyore.

Everyone looked high and low, but the jacket was nowhere to be found. The sun was much lower in the sky when the friends all gathered back at the bush to tell Christopher Robin the sad news. Just then, Piglet spotted something on the ground.

"It's a marble!" Piglet said, holding a shiny blue ball.
"Oh, that's nice. But we're looking for a jacket," Pooh said.
Rabbit borrowed Christopher Robin's notebook and wrote down
MARBUL. "This could be a clue," he said importantly.

"Yes, it could, Rabbit," Christopher Robin said excitedly. "That marble was in my jacket pocket!"

Just then, Owl, who was flying overhead, spotted something else. It was a handkerchief that had also been in the jacket pocket.

Before long, the friends had found some kite string, four lemon drops, and three more marbles from the jacket.

"These clues must lead somewhere," Rabbit said.

"They're leading to my house!" cried Roo.

"Yes, yes. Now let's review," Owl interrupted, peering over Rabbit's shoulder. "Piglet found the blue marble near the bush where we last saw the jacket."

"Good work, Piglet," Pooh said to his friend.

"Then Owl flew overhead, as only Owl can do, and he spotted the handkerchief in the meadow," Piglet said.

"Yes, and Eeyore found kite string in the thistles," Rabbit added.

"Now we're working like a team, Buddy Boys!" Tigger said.

"Wasn't it amazing how Pooh's tummy led him right to the lemon drops—one, two, three, four—just like that?" Roo cried.

Pooh couldn't help looking a little bit proud. "Just doing what my tummy does best," he said.

"Roo found the red marble," Christopher Robin said.

"And slipped on it," Eeyore added.

"Yes, and when I fell down, Tigger bent down to help me up and he spotted the other marbles up ahead!" Roo said happily.

"Isn't it wonderful how we all have our own special ways of helping?" Piglet said.

"Yep, and when we put them all together, we make quite a team!" Pooh cried.

"There's just one problem with all of this great teamwork,"
Rabbit said. "We still haven't found Christopher Robin's jacket!"
"And now we're lost," Eeyore sighed.
"We're not lost, Eeyore," Christopher Robin said.

"We're almost at my house!" Roo cried out.

"Mighty peculiar," Rabbit muttered. "Follow me!" And Rabbit marched right up to Roo's front door and knocked.

"Come in," Kanga called from inside.

"Aha!" Rabbit said, as he stepped inside and spotted the blue jacket with gold buttons on Kanga's lap.

"I saw you snag your jacket on the bush, dear," Kanga said to Christopher Robin. "I thought I would just sew it up for you."

Christopher Robin thanked Kanga, and everyone cheered.
"We found it! We found the jacket!" Roo squealed.
"We sure did," Christopher Robin said, smiling. "But then, we can do just about anything when we work together as a team!"

A LESSON A DAY POOH'S WAY

Working together

gets the job done!